Karen's Field Day

**Other books by
Ann M. Martin**

P. S. Longer Letter Later
(written with Paula Danziger)
Leo the Magnificat
Rachel Parker, Kindergarten Show-off
Eleven Kids, One Summer
Ma and Pa Dracula
Yours Turly, Shirley
Ten Kids, No Pets
With You and Without You
Me and Katie (the Pest)
Stage Fright
Inside Out
Bummer Summer

For older readers:

Missing Since Monday
Just a Summer Romance
Slam Book

THE BABY-SITTERS CLUB series
THE BABY-SITTERS CLUB mysteries
THE KIDS IN MS. COLMAN'S CLASS series
BABY-SITTERS LITTLE SISTER series
(see inside book covers for a complete listing)

Little Sister

Karen's Field Day
Ann M. Martin

Illustrations by Susan Crocca Tang

A
LITTLE APPLE
PAPERBACK

SCHOLASTIC INC.
New York Toronto London Auckland Sydney
Mexico City New Delhi Hong Kong

ISBN 0-590-50060-0

12 11 10 9 8 7 6 5 4 3 2   9/9 0 1 2 3 4/0

Printed in the U.S.A.   40
First Scholastic printing, April 1999

The author gratefully acknowledges
Gabrielle Charbonnet
for her help
with this book.

1

Karen and Andrew

"Look what I found!" I said. I was helping Daddy in the big-house garden. It was a beautiful April morning. The sun was shining and the birds were singing. The flowers were just beginning to bloom.

I held out my trowel. "A big fat worm!" I said.

"Wow!" said my little brother, Andrew. "Some worm!"

"Do not hurt it, Karen," said Daddy. "When you are done looking at the worm,

put it back in the dirt. Worms are good for the soil, you know."

"I know," I said. "I will not hurt it. I like worms."

It is true. I do like worms. I like all animals. (Well, almost all. I am not fond of mosquitoes.)

Oops, I have not even told you who I am yet. My name is Karen Brewer. I am seven years old. I live in Stoneybrook, Connecticut. I am in Ms. Colman's second-grade class at Stoneybrook Academy. I have blonde hair and blue eyes and freckles. I will tell you more about myself soon.

"I am getting hot," said Andrew. He wiped his face on his jacket sleeve.

"Gardening is good exercise," said Daddy. He pulled a weed out by the roots.

"Then I will work in the garden every day," I said. "I need to get in shape for Field Day." I flexed my arm muscle.

"What is Field Day?" asked Andrew.

"What is Field Day?" I repeated. I could not believe he did not know what Field Day was. (Sometimes I forget that Andrew is only four going on five.)

"Field Day is the most fun day of the whole school year," I said. "There are races and contests and games, all outdoors. And there are prizes. This year the kid who earns the most points in each class wins a gift certificate to Phil's Sporting Goods Shop. And after the prizes are given out, there is a big picnic."

"That sounds like fun," said Andrew.

"Oh, it is fun," I said. "And you are invited to watch the races and come to the picnic afterward."

"Really?" Andrew looked very pleased.

"Sure," I said. "Everyone's families will be there. Daddy will be there."

"Yup," said Daddy. "I would not miss Karen's Field Day for all the tea in China."

I did not know what Chinese tea had to do with it. But I just said, "And Mommy will be there too."

"Gosh!" said Andrew. "Daddy and

Mommy at the same time? Field Day must be very special."

"It is," I said.

You might be wondering what is so amazing about both my mommy and my daddy coming to Field Day. It is because they do not do many things together. And now I will tell you why.

2

The Story of My Families

A long time ago, when I was little, Mommy, Daddy, Andrew, and I lived together in Daddy's big house. Then Mommy and Daddy started to argue a lot. They told Andrew and me that they loved us very much, but they did not love each other anymore. And they could not live together anymore. They decided to get a divorce.

Mommy moved into her own little house in another neighborhood. Andrew and I moved with her. Daddy stayed in the big house, because he had grown up there.

After awhile Mommy and Daddy got married again. But not to each other. Mommy married a nice man named Seth Engle. He is my stepfather now. Seth has a dog, Midgie, and a cat, Rocky. So now at the little house live Mommy; Seth; Andrew; me; Midgie; Rocky; my pet rat, Emily Junior; and Andrew's hermit crab, Bob.

At the big house are many, many people. Daddy married a nice woman named Elizabeth Thomas. She is our stepmother. She has four children of her own. They are Sam and Charlie, who are practically grown-ups. (They are in high school.) There is Kristy, who is thirteen and the best stepsister ever. There is David Michael, who is seven like me, but an older seven. (He does not go to my school.)

Awhile ago, Daddy and Elizabeth adopted my little sister, Emily Michelle, from the faraway country of Vietnam. Emily is two and a half. She is gigundoly cute. I named my pet rat after her. The other pets at the big house are Shannon, David Michael's enormous Bernese mountain dog puppy; Pumpkin, a little black kitten; Crystal Light the Second, my goldfish; and Goldfishie, Andrew's trout (ha-ha).

There are so many people and pets at the big house that Elizabeth's mother, Nannie, moved in too, to help take care of everyone. Nannie has a candy-making business at the big house. Sometimes I help her. I even helped her win a cooking contest once!

Now Andrew and I live at the little house one month and at the big house the next month. (April was a big-house month.) This is a very good system because it means we get to spend lots of time with everyone in both our families.

When Andrew and I move from one house to the other, Emily Junior and Bob move back and forth with us. Most of my stuff does not move back and forth, though. That would be too complicated. Instead, I just have two of lots of things. I have two stuffed cats, two bicycles, two pairs of pink sneakers. . . . I even have two pieces of

Tickly, my special blanket — one for each house. Also, I have two houses, two mommies, two daddies, two pairs of glasses (one for reading and one for the rest of the time), and two best friends.

Andrew and I have two of so many things that I made up nicknames for us. I call us Andrew Two-Two and Karen Two-Two. (I got the idea from a book Ms. Colman read to my class. It was called *Jacob Two-Two Meets the Hooded Fang*.)

There! That just about does it. Of course, there is a lot more to know about me. For example, I am not very shy. But that is enough for now.

3

A New Class Project

"Class, I have an announcement to make," said Ms. Colman on Monday morning.

I sat up straight in my chair to listen. Ms. Colman's Surprising Announcements are always very exciting. They are one reason she is my favorite teacher.

"We are going to begin a project about writing, history, and research," said Ms. Colman.

I could not help wiggling in my chair. The project sounded fabulous already. And I was sure I would be good at it. After all, I love writing. (I am an excellent speller.) I love history. And I love finding out about new things. I could not wait to hear what the project would be.

"What is it, Ms. Colman?" I burst out. (Actually, I kind of shouted it.) "What are we going to do?"

"Indoor voice, Karen," Ms. Colman reminded me. Sometimes she has to remind me about my indoor voice three or four times in a single day. But she is never mean about it. That is another reason Ms. Colman is the best teacher ever. "And you forgot to raise your hand."

I raised my hand and waved it wildly in the air.

"Yes, Karen?" Ms. Colman called on me.

"What is our project going to be?" I asked in an indoor voice.

Ms. Colman smiled.

"We will be working on a family-history project," said Ms. Colman. "Now, many history books are mostly about famous men.

But women are a part of history too. For your project, you will ask your parents, grandparents, or other relatives about women from your families' pasts. Then you will each write a report about your most interesting female ancestor."

Hands shot up all around the room.

"Does the woman have to be famous?" asked Sara Ford.

"Does she have to be dead?" asked Hank Reubens.

"What if the woman is not an American?" called Omar Harris.

Ms. Colman held up her hands. "Hold on, hold on," she said. "Those are all good questions. She does not have to be famous, just interesting. She can still be alive. And she does not have to be American. Any other questions?"

No one raised a hand.

"Good," said Ms. Colman. "To help you get started, I have put together some sample questions to ask your parents or grandparents or aunts and uncles." Ms. Colman passed out a sheet of paper.

Women from My Family's History
Sample Questions to Ask a Relative
1. When you were a child, what woman in our family do you remember your parents talking about?
2. What was she known for?
3. When and where did she live?
4. How were stories about her passed down in the family?
5. Did you ever meet her? If not, would you like to have met her?

"Your reports are due the Monday after next," said Ms. Colman. "We will take turns presenting them to the rest of the class. And I will select several to put up on our workboard."

Our workboard is on the wall. We tape our best work there. Across the top is a big banner Ms. Colman made. It says, WE ARE DOING GREAT WORK! I looove having my work put on the workboard.

I folded up the sheet of sample questions that Ms. Colman had handed out. I put it in my backpack to take home to the big house.

I could hardly wait to get home and ask Daddy about the Brewer women. I was sure there would be many, many glamorous and exciting ancestors to choose from. I wondered if maybe we had any real princesses in our family. We do not now, of course. But maybe we did a long time ago. Or maybe one of our ancestors was a famous woman scientist who invented something wonderful, like ice cream.

And that was only on Daddy's side of the family. Mommy's family, the Packetts, would probably be just as full of gigundoly interesting women. How would I ever choose? I would have to play eenie, meenie, minie, moe. This project was going to be so, so much fun.

4

Hannie and Nancy

I have not told you about my two best friends yet. They are in Ms. Colman's class with me. Their names are Hannie Papadakis and Nancy Dawes.

Hannie lives across the street and one house down from the big house. Nancy lives next door to the little house. We have all been best friends for a long time. In fact, Hannie, Nancy, and I call ourselves the Three Musketeers. This has nothing to do with the candy bar (I like M&M's more —

they are nibblier). It is because the Three Musketeers' motto was "All for one and one for all." It is our motto too.

Today at lunch we sat together, like we always do. Tuna melt was the school lunch. If you have never had a tuna melt, you might not expect one to be very good. You might think, *Cheese and fish together? Yuck!* Well, you would be wrong. Tuna melts are delicious.

"Are you going to enter all the events on Field Day, Karen?" asked Nancy.

I swallowed a big bite of cheesy tuna. "Sure!" I said. "What about you?"

"I do not think so," said Nancy. "Last year in the wheelbarrow race I was the wheelbarrow. My hands slipped and I fell on my chin. That was not much fun."

"I think I remember that," said Hannie. "Someone was pushing you too fast."

"Well, I was not hurt badly," said Nancy. "And it was partly my fault for slipping. But I do not want to be in the wheelbarrow race again this year."

16

"What if you are the pusher, and someone else is the wheelbarrow?" I suggested.

Nancy thought. "That would be okay," she decided. "But who would I push?" She looked at Hannie and me.

Hannie did not say anything. Neither did I. I did not want to fall on my face. I did not think Hannie did either.

Nancy looked disappointed.

I did not want Nancy to be disappointed. I would have to think about it some more. In the meantime, I decided to change the subject.

"Our woman ancestor project will be fun," I said. "I cannot wait to ask my mommy and daddy about famous women in my family."

"Me neither!" said Hannie. "But I already know who I am going to write about. My great-aunt Sofia Papadakis was the first female brain surgeon in America. She helped save a lot of really sick people."

Wow! A brain surgeon. I wondered if there were any brain surgeons in my family.

"I know who I will write about too," said Nancy. "My great-grandmother spied for the French freedom fighters in World War Two. She was captured by the Germans. They sent her to prison. Then she escaped. After the war, she received a medal from the mayor of Paris."

Double wow! A war-hero spy who went to jail and got a medal.

Now I was really excited. If Hannie and Nancy had these cool women in their families, I bet my family had women astronauts, or famous athletes, or brilliant artists.

My only question was: If there were so many great women in my family, why had I not heard of any of them? Were Mommy and Daddy just being modest?

5

Daddy's Story

" 'Bye, Hannie!" I called as I stepped off the bus. When I am at the big house, I ride the school bus home with Hannie. When I am at the little house, I ride home with Nancy. It is very convenient always to live close to a best friend.

I raced home to find Daddy. I wanted to ask him about the Brewer women right away. Luckily, Daddy works out of an office right in our house, so I would not have to wait for him to come home from work. We are not supposed to disturb him unless it is an emergency, but I knew he would be excited about my project.

I slammed the front door (by accident) and threw my books down at the bottom of the stairs. "I am home!" I yelled. I pounded past the stairs toward Daddy's office.

"Daddy, Daddy!" I called, tearing off my jacket.

"What?" said Daddy. He came bounding out of his office. "What is the matter, Karen? Is there some kind of emergency?"

"Yes!" I said.

"What is it?" Daddy looked almost as excited as I was feeling. "Is someone injured?" He looked around to see if someone was lying hurt on the ground.

"No!" I said. "I have to find out about famous Brewer women for a class project!"

Daddy was silent for a moment. "There is no emergency?"

"Well, no one is hurt," I admitted. "This is more of a homework emergency. I want to get started on my project right away. After all, it is due in two weeks."

Daddy looked at me. He looked at his watch. He took a deep breath. "Well, it is time for a little break anyway," he said. "I will be happy to help you out, Karen. But next time, do not frighten me by screaming like that, okay?"

"Okay," I said.

We walked into his office together. (I did not even get a snack first. That is how excited I was.) Daddy sat down at his desk. I sat in a big comfy chair across from him and unzipped my backpack. First I pulled out Ms. Colman's suggested questions. Then I opened my notebook to a fresh sheet and took out a sharpened pencil.

" 'When you were a child,' " I read aloud, " 'what woman in our family do you remember your parents talking about?' "

"Hmm," Daddy said thoughtfully. He leaned back in his chair and looked at the ceiling. "There were so many."

"Really?" I asked eagerly. Here we go! I thought.

"Oh yes," said Daddy. He smiled. "For instance, there was Great-aunt Josephine Adelaide Brewer. She was the talk of the town."

"The talk of the town!" I said, writing down her name. "Great! What was she famous for? Was she an important scientist?"

"Oh, heavens, no," said Daddy, chuckling.

I thought about Hannie's and Nancy's ancestors. "Was she a war hero? A brilliant doctor?"

Daddy laughed out loud. "No, nothing like that," he said. A faraway look came into his eyes. "Great-aunt Josephine was famous for her lavish parties. Why, I remember my parents telling me about how every Independence Day, Great-aunt Josephine would invite half the town of West Dudley, Massachusetts, to her house. It was the social event of the season. And fancy! The men wore white linen suits, and the women wore gowns. They played croquet on the lawn.

Live musicians serenaded everyone from the front porch."

Fancy parties? Croquet? Musicians?

I like parties as much as the next person (probably more, in fact), but still . . . was that all Great-aunt Josephine was known for?

"Did any famous people ever come to Great-aunt Josephine's parties?" I asked. "Movie stars? Gangsters?"

"Well, I believe the mayor of West Dudley usually attended," Daddy said. "And he did not go to many parties, they say. Here." He opened a drawer in his desk and started looking through a file. "I believe I have an old photo of Aunt Josephine."

"Um, that is okay, Daddy," I said. "I do not need to see her picture just yet." Aunt Josephine did not seem like report material. I mean, if Hannie and Nancy were writing about war heroes and brain surgeons, there was no way I was going to write about a woman who threw parties.

Daddy was gazing at an old brownish photograph and sighing. Quietly I slipped out of his office.

Oh, well, I thought. There was always Mommy's side of the family.

6

Gym Class

Tweeet! Mrs. Mackey blew her whistle to get the class's attention. Mrs. Mackey is Stoneybrook Academy's gym teacher. She knows all about sports and games and stuff like that.

Tweeet! Mrs. Mackey likes to blow her whistle.

"Listen up, people!" she called out.

We were on the playground. Mrs. Mackey had divided us into teams. Each team had been practicing shooting basketballs. I had almost made a basket three times. Hannie had almost made one twice. Nancy had actually made one. I really wanted to make one too.

"Gym is almost over," said Mrs. Mackey when she had everyone's attention. "Before we go inside, I want to talk to you about Field Day."

"Yea!" we all shouted. Everyone loves Field Day. I forgot about basketball.

"There will be eight events," Mrs. Mackey said. She ticked them off on her fingers. "Fifty-meter sprint. Four-hundred meter run. Four-person relay race. Standing long jump. Sack race. Wheelbarrow race. Three-legged race. Water-balloon toss."

Everyone started talking at once about the Field Day events. We could not help it. It was too exciting.

Tweeet! "Ten points will be given for finishing first in any event. Five points for second. And two points for third," said Mrs. Mackey. "Whoever has the most points in each grade at the end of the day will win a gift certificate to Phil's Sporting Goods."

"Yea!" we shouted.

Tweeet! "Any questions?" Mrs. Mackey asked.

Nobody raised a hand.

Tweeet! "Class dismissed."

Ms. Colman led us back inside the school building to our classroom. I like Mrs. Mackey. And I like gym class. But I am glad that Ms. Colman does not blow a whistle at us all the time.

During afternoon recess, Nancy, Hannie, and I huddled to talk about Field Day. We wanted to plan our strategy. The Three Musketeers were determined to win as many points as possible.

"We should all enter all of the events," I said. "That way there's a better chance that one of us will win."

"We will need a fourth person for the relay race," Hannie pointed out.

"I will ask Sara Ford," said Nancy. "She is a fast runner."

"Good idea," I said. "Now, who will team

up for the three-legged race?"

"I will do it with you," said Hannie. "Is that okay, Nancy?"

Nancy nodded. "I guess so. I will ask Sara if she wants to team up with me for that race too."

"Great," said Hannie. "And since I will run the three-legged race with Karen, you two can do the wheelbarrow race together. Maybe I will try to get a boy to do that one with me."

"Okay," I said. "Nancy, who will be the wheelbarrow? You or me?" I had a feeling I knew what she would say.

"I do not want to be the wheelbarrow," said Nancy. She rubbed her chin, as if it still hurt from last year.

I had had a chance to think about being the wheelbarrow. I did not really want to be the wheelbarrow. But I decided I would, to make Nancy happy. That is what friends do.

"Okay." I sighed. "I will be the wheelbarrow. You may push me. I will try hard not to fall."

Nancy smiled. "Thanks, Karen," she said. "I will be careful not to push too fast."

"Push just fast enough to win," I said.

Nancy nodded.

"And that leaves Nancy and me together for the water-balloon toss," said Hannie. "I hope it is warm outside on Field Day." (People always get wet during the water-balloon toss.)

"Me too," I said. "I think I will ask Ricky Torres to be my water-balloon partner." (Ricky is my pretend husband. We were married on the playground one day.)

The Three Musketeers grinned at one another. We were all set. Field Day was going to be so much fun!

Vowing to Win

Nancy, Hannie, and I were just about to go inside when Pamela Harding walked by.

I do not like to say mean things about people, so I will not say anything about Pamela. Even if she deserves it. Pamela has been my best enemy ever since she came to Stoneybrook Academy.

Pamela was talking to her best friends, Jannie Gilbert and Leslie Morris.

"I cannot wait to win the most second-grade points on Field Day," Pamela said in a very loud voice. "I love Phil's Sporting

Goods Shop. I already know how I am going to spend the gift certificate."

"Really?" asked Jannie. "What are you going to buy?"

"Yes, what?" said Leslie. (They always go along with whatever Pamela says.)

"Pamela is not going to buy anything," I called over to them. "Because she is not going to win on Field Day."

"Oh yeah?" said Pamela. "What makes you think that?"

"I think that because it is true," I said.

"Well, you are wrong, Karen," said Pamela. "I am going to win. And I am going to buy a million pom-pom socks." She turned to Jannie and Leslie. "I saw the cutest pom-pom socks at Phil's the other day. They were in all different colors. With the gift certificate, I will be able to buy a pair to match just about every outfit in my — "

"Pom-pom socks!" I said. "That is the silliest thing I have ever heard."

Pamela crossed her arms over her chest.

"It is not! What would you buy if you

won?" she asked. "Which you are not going to do anyway."

"Am too!" I said. "And when I win, I will not waste my gift certificate on goofy pom-pom socks."

I did not know what I would spend a gift certificate on at a sporting-goods store. I had not thought about it yet. Maybe swim flippers, or new roller skates. Definitely not pom-pom socks.

"If *you* wore them, they *would* be goofy pom-pom socks," said Pamela. "When *I* wear them, they will be stylish and fashion-able pom-pom socks."

Pamela stuck out her tongue and flounced off. Jannie and Leslie flounced off after her.

Pamela is such a meanie-mo. I might as well tell you. After all, you have probably figured it out for yourself.

I turned to Hannie and Nancy. "We will show Pamela. One of us will win that gift certificate. We will share whatever we get. And we will not waste it on pom-pom socks."

"Cool!" said Hannie.

"We will not let Pamela beat us," said Nancy.

"Let's make a Three Musketeers vow," I said. "Pamela Harding will not win Field Day — no matter what."

I stuck my hand out palm down and said, "All for one."

Nancy put her hand on mine, and Hannie put her hand on Nancy's.

"And one for all!" we shouted together.

The Three P's

"I suppose you are wondering why I asked you to come over today," I said.

It was Wednesday, after school. Nancy had ridden to my house on the school bus. Her mommy would pick her up later. Hannie had crossed the street to my house, instead of going home. After Nannie had fixed the three of us a snack, we had come out to the backyard. Now we were sitting in the farthest corner of the yard. We would be very private there.

"To play?" Nancy guessed.

"Nope," I said.

"To pull up weeds?" said Hannie.

"Nope."

Nancy and Hannie looked at each other. "We give up," said Nancy.

"We have to come up with a surefire plan for winning Field Day," I told them.

They nodded.

"Okay, I have a plan," said Hannie. "How about if we run faster, jump longer, and toss water balloons farther than anyone else? That should do the trick."

Nancy giggled.

"I am serious," I said. "I have been thinking about this a lot. I have realized that we will not win Field Day without the three P's." (I had heard about the three P's from Sam and Charlie. They play sports in high school.)

"What are the three P's?" asked Nancy. (She was not giggling now.)

"Preparation. Practice. Performance," I said, feeling important.

"Ooh," said Nancy. "That sounds good. What does it mean?"

"I am glad you asked that," I said seriously. I felt like a football coach giving a pep talk at halftime. I stood up and started pacing back and forth. "First is Preparation. That means exercising. Working out. Building up our strength. We will have to whip ourselves into shape." I pounded my fist into my hand.

"Yes!" said Hannie and Nancy.

"Then there is Practice," I said. "We have to improve our skills in the events. Especially the tough ones, like the three-legged race and the wheelbarrow race. We must master the skills and techniques." That is what Sam said his coach had said. It sounded terrific.

"All right! Master those skills!" shouted Nancy and Hannie.

"Last is Performance," I said. "When Field Day comes, Preparation will give us endurance. Practice will give us skill. And a winning Performance will give us the Field Day championship — *and* a gift certificate to Phil's Sporting Goods."

"Yea!" Hannie and Nancy leaped up. They jumped up and down and slapped high fives. I had done a good job of getting them excited.

"Now let's go win one for the Gipper!" I shouted. (I do not know who the Gipper is. But I know that coaches always want their teams to win one for him.)

That very afternoon, Hannie and Nancy and I started our Preparation. We ran around the big house four times. We did twenty sit-ups. We did thirty leg lifts. We did forty jumping jacks.

We flopped down on the grass, panting. We were pooped.

"Is that enough Preparation, Karen?" Nancy asked breathlessly. "I need to rest."

"That is enough for now," I said. I stood up. "Come on, Musketeers. Practice comes next."

I went inside and found three bandannas. When I came back, Hannie and Nancy were still lying next to each other on the grass. But they were not panting so hard.

I sat between my friends, with my left leg next to Hannie's right leg. Then I tied our ankles, knees, and thighs together with the bandannas. (Not too tightly.)

"Okay, teammate," I said. I wished I had a whistle, like Mrs. Mackey did. "Up and at 'em! Get a move on!"

Hannie and I heaved ourselves off the grass. We hobbled a few steps, but we were not moving together. After a few seconds, Hannie said, "Whoa!" and flailed her arms. She toppled sideways onto the grass, pulling me down on top of her.

"Oof!" I said.

What I would have given for a whistle just then. I could see that for our Performance to be good enough to win Field Day, we were going to need a lot more Preparation and Practice.

9

Mommy's Story

On Friday I ate dinner at the little house, even though it was a big-house month. I did this for two reasons:

1. I wanted to borrow an exercise tape from Mommy.

2. I wanted to talk to Mommy about interesting Packett women. (Packett was Mommy's last name before she married Daddy. Then it became Brewer. When she married Seth, she changed her last name to Engle. My name is still Brewer.)

Mommy had made a special meal that she knew I would like.

"Yum!" I said. "Spaghetti and meatballs! Crusty bread and snap peas! My favorites." Mommy smiled at me. It felt a little weird to be at the little house without Andrew. Usually we are here together.

After dinner (orange sherbet for dessert, yum) I sat with Mommy in the living room. I took out the sheet of sample questions that Ms. Colman had given us. I read out loud, " 'Number one. When you were a child, what woman in our family do you remember your parents talking about?' "

"Goodness, there were a lot," Mommy said.

"Really?" I asked. Great! I would not have to use Daddy's great-aunt Josephine.

"Let's see," said Mommy. "There was my mother's cousin Livia. She loved to fish. She would go out in her hip boots and cast flies with her six brothers. Catch more than all the boys put together too. Once she caught fourteen largemouth bass in one afternoon. It was a record for Winslow's Fishing Hole."

"That is interesting, sort of," I said. "But I was hoping for something a little more . . . exciting."

"How about Great-aunt Harriet?" said Mommy. "She was a real character. The story in the family goes that when her dad died, she took over the family business — running a bookmaking service!"

"She was a book publisher?" I asked. "Gosh."

Mommy laughed. "No, Karen, a bookmaking service is where people go to place bets, like on racehorses. It is not legal. Great-aunt Harriet was a bookie. Or so the family legend has it."

"A bookie!" I exclaimed. "You mean she was a criminal?"

"Well, technically, I guess she was," said Mommy. "She was sort of a nice criminal. She never went to prison."

I thought about Nancy's relative, the war hero who had gone to jail for spying. There was no way I was going to write about my relative who had not gone to jail for taking illegal bets.

"Anyone else?" I asked. I was beginning to think there was a reason why I had never heard of any important Packett or Brewer women. "Anybody famous?"

"Certainly," said Mommy. "There was my aunt Patsy. She was famous for her big feet. She had bigger feet than her brother — and he was six foot three. And Granny Nolan could drink water and whistle at the same time — with or without her dentures in!"

Now I was feeling very discouraged. Even Daddy's party-throwing aunt was better than the whistling granny.

"And of course there was Edna Milton," Mommy said.

"Who was she?" I asked grimly.

"Edna was born in London, around the turn of the century," said Mommy. "She lived at Highgate Hall, one of the grand houses of England."

"Really? A grand house?" I perked up

and started scribbling notes. I had had no idea that one of my relatives was a rich English lady! I wondered if Edna Milton had had a title, like duchess or baroness. And if Edna had had a title, and I was related to her, was it possible that I might have a title too?

I could see it now: Karen Brewer, Duchess of Stoneybrook. Her Royal Majesty Karen, Princess of Connecticut.

Then Mommy said, "Edna was a servant at Highgate Hall."

"A servant!" The Princess of Connecticut disappeared.

"Yes," said Mommy. "I believe she was a scullery maid."

I stopped taking notes. "Gee. Well, did she run off with the rich son? And his parents were furious? And they had to live in a foreign country because his family would not speak to them?"

"Um, no," said Mommy. "Edna ran off with the under-gardener and opened a flower shop in London. The shop failed, though. So Edna and Nigel, I believe his name was, set sail for America."

Mommy shook her head slowly and looked sad.

"What happened?" I asked.

"Their ship went down," said Mommy. "They drowned before they ever saw America."

Their ship went down? I took a deep breath. Could it be? "Was the ship the *Titanic*?" I asked hopefully.

"Oh, no," said Mommy. "It was the *Beulah May*."

Beulah May? Never heard of it.

I sighed a long sigh. I folded up my sheet of notes and stuck it in my pocket.

"Thank you, Mommy," I said. "You have been a big help." That was not true, but I did not want to hurt Mommy's feelings. I did not want to tell her that her female relatives were even worse than Daddy's female relatives.

"You are welcome, Karen," said Mommy. "If you want to know any more about the Packett women, just ask."

"Okay," I said. "But I think I have heard enough already."

10

Aerobics Is Not for Wimps

The next morning the other Musketeers came over to the big house. We went into the family room.

I was wearing a leotard, tights, leg warmers, and a headband. My hair was in a ponytail. I had draped a small towel around my neck. Hannie and Nancy were in their workout clothes too.

"Ready to sweat?" I asked. "Ready to get in shape? Ready to beat Pamela Harding?"

"Ready!" said Hannie.

"Go for it!" said Nancy.

I held up the aerobics tape I had borrowed from Mommy the night before. It was called *Earn the Burn!* On the cover was a picture of a nice-looking blonde woman with a ponytail. She was wearing workout clothes. I thought she looked sort of like me, without the glasses.

I popped the tape into the VCR. Hannie, Nancy, and I took our positions and got ready.

Jazzy music started up, and the blonde woman appeared. She started touching her toes and saying, "Come on! You can do it! Earn the burn!"

Quickly Hannie, Nancy, and I started touching our toes too.

Then the woman started swinging her arms from side to side. She said, "Here we go! Here we go! Earn the burn!"

We swung our arms from side to side.

Then she did waist bends. ("Earn the burn!")

We did waist bends.

I was beginning to feel a little tired and

sweaty. I could hear Hannie and Nancy panting next to me. This was a great workout. We were definitely earning the burn.

The music slowed and faded out. I thought that was the end of the tape. I started to walk toward the VCR.

Then the woman said something really surprising: "That completes our five-minute warm-up. Now we will begin the workout."

"What?" said Nancy. "The exercises have not even begun yet?"

"I guess not," I said. "Aerobics is not for wimps, you know."

The music started up again, only faster and louder this time.

I jumped back to my spot.

The woman started jogging in place.

We jogged in place.

She kicked her legs in the air, as if she were part of a chorus line.

We kicked our legs in the air. (Not as high as the woman did. Nancy's feet were hardly leaving the ground.)

The woman did deep knee bends.

We did not-so-deep knee bends. (Nancy did three, then fell over onto the rug.)

The woman jogged in place some more.

We jogged in place. (Hannie sort of stood there, lifting her heels every now and then.)

The woman did jumping jacks.

We did jumping jacks. (Hannie did two, then collapsed in a heap.)

All the while the woman was smiling and shouting, "Earn the burn! Earn the burn! Earn the burn!"

Finally the woman dived onto her hands and started doing pushups.

I had had enough. I picked up the remote and clicked her off. Then I flopped down between Hannie and Nancy. My face felt hot and sweaty. I could hardly breathe. I decided maybe aerobics was not right for us.

"I think I will give Mommy back her tape the next time I see her," I said.

Nancy and Hannie nodded.

"I think that is a good idea," said Nancy. "We can just do our own exercises."

"Yeah," I agreed.

11

Pamela, Schmamela

By Monday I was feeling pretty good about the Three Musketeers' progress with the three P's. Despite the aerobics disaster, we were becoming Prepared.

We spent all day Sunday Practicing our events.

With two more weeks of Preparation and Practice, I was sure we would be ready to Perform up to our Potential. (Hey, I had thought of a fourth P! I would have to tell Sam and Charlie about it.)

On the playground before school I sized

up the competition. Some of the boys, such as Hank Reubens and Bobby Gianelli, were pretty fast. Some, such as Ian Johnson and Chris Lamar, were not.

My pretend husband, Ricky, is sometimes fast and sometimes slow. When we play tag and I chase him, he is slow. But when he chases me, he is fast. I am not sure why this is.

I knew that even though Hank and Bobby are fast, they were not going to win Field Day. A lot of the events would require teamwork. And I was sure Hank and Bobby were not Practicing the way the Three Musketeers were.

Of the girls, I figured the most competition would come from Sara Ford. She was pretty tall and could run fast. (She had agreed to be the Three Musketeers' fourth teammate in the relay race.) We would have to watch out for her.

The other girls — Tammy and Terri Barkan, Jannie Gilbert, Audrey Green, Addie Sidney, and Leslie Morris — would not be a problem. I knew we could beat them.

Oh, yes. There was one other girl in the class. Pamela Harding.

I scanned the school yard. There she was. Sure, she could run fast and jump far. She was, I had to admit, pretty good at gym — even if she mostly exercised her mouth. But there was no way she was going to win Field Day. No way. I just would not allow it to happen.

And besides, we had been Preparing ourselves and Practicing. Was Pamela doing either of those things? No. The only P she was doing was Prancing around looking silly.

"Wow," said Nancy. She was watching Pamela too.

"Wow what?" I asked.

"Wow, look at Pamela."

"She is just prancing around like a silly elf," I said.

"She is not prancing," said Nancy. "She is aerobicizing. I heard her talking about it with Jannie. Pamela has been going with her mother to an aerobics class. She is showing Jannie the routine they do in class."

My eyes widened. I watched Pamela closely. She no longer looked like a silly prancing elf. She was kicking her legs high in the air. She was jumping up and down. She was leaping from side to side.

Pamela reminded me of the blonde woman on Mommy's exercise tape. Pamela had a *lot* of energy. I even thought I heard her shout "Earn the burn!" once or twice.

Uh-oh. Pamela was going to be harder to beat than I had thought. The Three Musketeers would have to Prepare ourselves and Practice even harder if our Performance was going to be good enough to win.

Workout Diary

When I told Kristy about getting ready
for Field Day, she suggested I keep a Workout Diary, so that I would know how much
Preparation I was getting. (Kristy is a gigundoly great athlete.) It was a good idea. I got
excited about exercising all over again. Here
is how my week went:

TUESDAY MORNING. LEAPED OUT OF BED AS SOON AS
ALARM WENT OFF. DID TWENTY JUMPING JACKS — FELT
GREAT. ATE CEREAL, TOAST, JUICE, MILK. RAN
TO SCHOOL BUS STOP AS FAST AS I COULD. JOGGED

IN PLACE WHILE WAITING FOR BUS.

TUESDAY RECESS. TALKED WITH TWO MUSKETEERS. DID NOT WORK OUT — DID NOT WANT PAMELA HARD- ING TO KNOW OUR SECRET. BUT WE JUMPED ROPE EX- TRA HARD SO SNUCK IN A GOOD WORKOUT.

TUESDAY AFTER SCHOOL. RAN AROUND HOUSE SEVEN TIMES. DID FOUR PULL-UPS FROM LIMB OF MAPLE TREE IN BACKYARD. PRACTICED SACK RACE.

WEDNESDAY MORNING. LEAPED OUT OF BED. TWENTY JUMPING JACKS. BIG BREAKFAST. RAN TO BUS STOP, JOGGED IN PLACE.

WEDNESDAY RECESS. MET WITH 2 MS. MADE SURE P.H. WAS NOT WATCHING. PRACTICED STANDING LONG JUMP WHILE PRETENDING TO PLAY HOPSCOTCH. (CAN JUMP ALMOST MY HEIGHT!)

WEDNESDAY AFTER SCHOOL. TEN TIMES AROUND HOUSE. FOUR PULL-UPS. PRACTICED WHEELBARROW RACE WITH NANCY. FELL ON FACE THREE TIMES. GOT GRASS UP MY NOSE. DAVID MICHAEL SAW IT AND LAUGHED. IGNORED HIM. WILL HAVE TO WORK ON WHEELBARROW SOME MORE.

THURSDAY MORNING. LEAPED FROM BED. TWENTY J.J.S. GOOD BREAKFAST. RAN TO BUS.

THURSDAY RECESS. PLAYED RED-HOT PEPPER JUMP

ROPE WITH 2 MS. NO SIGN OF P.H.

THURSDAY AFTER SCHOOL. RAINING. RAN UP AND DOWN STAIRS INSIDE UNTIL NANNIE TOLD ME TO QUIT MAKING ALL THAT RACKET.

FRIDAY MORNING. LEAPED, JUMPED, ATE, RAN.

FRIDAY RECESS. CLIMBED TO TOP OF JUNGLE GYM EIGHT TIMES. SAW P.H. SITTING UNDER TREE TALKING TO JANNIE AND LESLIE. EXERCISING NOTHING BUT HER MOUTH, HA! P.H. HAS NO IDEA THAT THE 3 MS ARE PREPARING AND PRACTICING FOR FIELD DAY.

FRIDAY AFTER SCHOOL. TWELVE HOUSE LAPS. SEVEN PULL-UPS. PRACTICED WHEELBARROW RACE WITH NANCY — DID NOT FALL ON FACE ONCE. AM GETTING TO BE PRETTY GOOD AT IT. P.H. IS NOT GOING TO KNOW WHAT HIT HER.

Well, that just about summed up my week. It was Prepare, Prepare, Prepare, with some Practice thrown in.

By Friday evening I was completely worn out. I went to bed at seven o'clock, right after dinner.

I was tired. But it was a good tired. I was getting in shape. I was doing all I could to get myself ready for Field Day. I pictured myself accepting the gift certificate from Ms. Colman. I pictured myself buying some cool sports equipment and sharing it with my friends. I fell asleep smiling.

13

Morning Sky

A body needs rest sometimes, to recover from working out. Afterward, when you start exercising again, you have more energy than ever. That is what Charlie told me.

So on Saturday I took it easy.

I went to Hannie's house. Nancy was there too. We were a little sore from all the exercise. We did quiet things that did not require much moving around. We read. We played with dolls. We drew. We talked. It was very pleasant. When you have good friends like Hannie and Nancy, you can have fun doing lots of different things. Even quiet things. (Usually I do not do so many quiet things.)

That night, after supper, I was sitting in the living room, still taking it easy. David Michael was lying on the floor, drawing airplanes. Daddy was sitting in his big chair, reading the paper. Elizabeth was starting a new needlework pillow. I felt very happy, surrounded by my family.

I curled up on the couch next to Elizabeth. I opened a book I had started at Hannie's house. Hannie had lent it to me. It was called *The Attic Mice*, by Ethel Pochocki. It was excellent.

I had just gotten to the part where the little boy mouse eats a cake of soap when I overheard Kristy talking on the phone.

I know it is rude to listen to other people's telephone conversations. But I was not doing it on purpose. I was minding my own business and could not help overhearing.

"It was the best movie I have ever seen," Kristy said into the phone.

I love movies. Which one was she talking about?

"Mary Anne, you have to go see *Morning Sky*," Kristy went on. "It is about a young woman pioneer, Eliza Hutton. She is traveling the Oregon Trail in a wagon train. Some bad guys in her group pick a fight with a couple of Native Americans. A Sioux Indian is killed. So the Sioux attack the wagon train in revenge and take Eliza prisoner."

Gosh, *Morning Sky* sounded exciting. I listened closely.

"Yes, that is right," said Kristy. "She is taken to live with the Sioux. They are not very nice to her at first, but they are not exactly mean either. Slowly she learns to speak their language. A handsome young man named Black Arrow is especially kind to her."

There was a pause for a moment. I could hardly wait for Kristy to tell the rest of the story.

"No," Kristy said, "Black Arrow was not one of the men who kidnapped her. He had

been against the idea of attacking the wagon train. Anyway, Black Arrow starts teaching Eliza the Sioux way of life. He gives her a Sioux name, Morning Sky, because she reminds him of the dawn. He even carves her a beautiful pendant that shows a rising sun. She falls in love with him."

How romantic, I thought.

"Then the U.S. Army attacks the Sioux, and Black Arrow gets ready to go to war. Morning Sky does not want him to go. He does not like war, but he has to defend his people. It is totally sad when he goes."

Golly, it did sound sad. I was getting teary eyed just hearing Kristy tell about it.

"Well, I will not tell you exactly how it ends," said Kristy. "I will just say that I cried hard, and Morning Sky finally makes it to Oregon. She goes on to marry a settler there and raise a family. But she never forgets Black Arrow. Though she is called Eliza, in her heart she knows her true name is Morning Sky. And when she is an old, old lady, she returns to the country of the Sioux and places Black Arrow's pendant on the battle-field where he died."

I closed up my book and placed it on my lap. I could not read any more anyway. Tears were running down my cheeks. What a wonderful, sad story!

14

Biggest Pumpkin

Mommy had told me about lots of the Packett women. But the only Brewer woman Daddy had told me about was Great-aunt Josephine, who threw parties. There had to be other Brewer women I could write about.

On Sunday morning I found Daddy working in the garden. He was planting flowers in the bed near the front steps.

"Daddy," I said, "I still do not have a woman ancestor to write about."

"Great-aunt Josephine was not good enough for you, eh?" he asked.

I shrugged.

"Okay, let me think." Daddy put down his trowel and took off his work gloves. "Well, my grandmother Ida Brewer was an interesting woman."

I opened my notebook and got ready to take notes. "Go on."

"I remember Grandma Ida telling me about how she traveled when she was young," said Daddy. "She took the grand tour of Europe. For three years she was on the road. She stayed in luxurious hotels in all the great capitals. She dined in the best restaurants."

"That sounds like a very nice vacation," I said. "But did Grandma Ida ever actually *do* anything?"

"She was an expert skier," Daddy said.

"Really?" I asked. "Did she go to the Olympics?"

"Well, no," Daddy said. "She was not that

expert. She gave lessons, though, when she came home to America. That is how she met my grandpa Bill. He was a student of hers in Vermont."

"Huh," I said. Being a ski instructor was kind of neat. But it was not *really* neat. And I wanted *really*, *really* neat.

"Anybody else?" I asked. "Were there any women who *did* anything? Won anything? Anything at all?"

Daddy thought for a long, long time. I began to lose hope.

Finally Daddy said, "Aunt Carol. She won a prize at the Ohio State Fair. Took first place for Biggest Pumpkin. This was back in nineteen sixty-six, I believe."

Biggest Pumpkin? Boo and bullfrogs!

I was getting desperate. "How about glamour? Mystery?" I asked.

"Glamour?" Daddy chuckled. "Well, Great-aunt Josephine was as glamorous as it got in our family, Karen. And you have already heard about her."

I sighed loudly.

70

"Okay, here is something," said Daddy. "I am not sure if it is true or not. But family legend had it that one of my mother's great-grandparents was a Native American woman. A Cherokee. She would have been your great-great-great-grandmother. So you may be a tiny bit Native American, Karen. That is kind of interesting, isn't it?"

"Yes!" I said. "So I am . . . what? One-quarter Native American?" I do not look very Native American.

"No, you would be, let me see . . ." said Daddy. He thought a moment. "You would be one one-hundred-and-twenty-eighth Native American. Maybe. I think."

My face fell. I had maybe three drops of Native American blood in me. No wonder I have blonde hair and blue eyes.

"I wish I could tell you more about our possible Cherokee ancestor," Daddy said. "But I do not know anything about her. She is just a story that has been handed down in the family. And now I am handing it to you."

"Thank you," I said politely.

Daddy pulled his work gloves back on and picked up his trowel. He started digging a hole to plant a flower in.

I had heard all the stories about Brewer women that I was going to hear.

15

Where Were the Brewer Spies?

Yikes! All of a sudden it was Sunday afternoon. I was in my room, sitting at my desk. My report on my female ancestor was due the *very next day*. And not only had I not started to write it yet, I did not even have anyone to write about. How had this happened? What was I going to do?

Not a single Brewer or Packett woman had done anything really great.

I thought about Hannie's brain surgeon

and Nancy's war hero. Those were impressive ancestors. What were my ancestors doing while the Papadakises and Daweses were curing cancer and winning wars? Having tea? Fixing their hair? Knitting?

Where were the brilliant Packett doctors? Where were the Brewer spies?

I thought about myself. I had helped Nannie win a cooking contest. I had caught an art thief in Chicago. I had become friends with a real live movie star. All this, and I am only seven!

I was a pretty outstanding kid, I thought. It was hard to believe that I did not come from more heroic stock.

There must be an explanation for my lack of great ancestors. Maybe I had plenty of them, but no one remembered them now. For example, whatever-her-name-was, my possibly Cherokee ancestor, could have been a truly fascinating woman. In fact, she probably had been. The problem was that no one remembered her story. Daddy did not even know her name.

The more I thought about it, the more it made sense. I must have had an ancestor who had led an amazing life. What's-her-name, my possibly Cherokee ancestor, could have been like Morning Sky, the woman in that movie Kristy saw.

Maybe my ancestor was not *born* Cherokee, but spent time among them and took a Cherokee name — just like in the movie. That would explain why Daddy was not sure whether she was Cherokee or not.

Yes, that was it. My ancestor must have been just like Morning Sky. I was sure of it.

I started to get excited about my ancestor who had lived among the Cherokees and fallen in love with a handsome warrior. It was such a sad, thrilling, romantic story. Much better than a boring old doctor or spy.

I took out a pencil and paper and started to write.

16

"My Ancestor," by Karen Brewer

The next day, Ms. Colman asked us to read our reports aloud in front of the class. I love reading aloud. This is what I read:

MY ANCESTOR, BY KAREN BREWER
THE MOST INTERESTING WOMAN IN MY FAMILY WAS NAMED EVENING STAR. THAT WAS HER CHEROKEE NAME. SHE WAS A PIONEER WOMAN DURING PIONEER TIMES. BEFORE THAT, SHE LIVED IN A BIG HOUSE IN ENGLAND CALLED HIGHGATE HALL. AFTER SHE CAME TO

AMERICA ON A SHIP THAT SANK, SHE WON A PRIZE FOR
GROWING THE BIGGEST PUMPKIN IN OHIO. LATER SHE
BECAME AN EXPERT SKIER AND ALMOST WENT TO THE
OLYMPICS. SHE COULD WHISTLE AND DRINK A GLASS OF
WATER AT THE SAME TIME. SHE WAS QUITE AN OUT-
STANDING WOMAN.

BUT THE MOST FASCINATING THING THAT HAPPENED
TO HER WAS WHEN SHE WAS TAKEN PRISONER BY NA-
TIVE AMERICANS. THE CHEROKEES DID THIS BECAUSE
THEY WERE MAD BECAUSE SOME PIONEERS HAD PICKED
A FIGHT WITH THEM. SO THEY KIDNAPPED MY ANCES-
TOR.

AT FIRST SHE WAS SAD. SHE MISSED HER FAMILY.
BUT THEN A KIND CHEROKEE NAMED RUNNING DEER
STARTED BEING NICE TO HER. HE WAS GIGUNDOLY
HANDSOME. HE GAVE HER CHEROKEE LESSONS. THEN
HE GAVE HER A NEW NAME, WHICH WAS EVENING
STAR. HE CALLED HER EVENING STAR BECAUSE SHE RE-
MINDED HIM OF A BEAUTIFUL STAR. HE CARVED A STAR-
SHAPED NECKLACE AND GAVE IT TO HER.

THEN RUNNING DEER HAD TO GO FIGHT AGAINST
THE ARMY. EVENING STAR WAS SO, SO SAD. BUT SHE
KNEW RUNNING DEER HAD TO GO. THEN HE WAS

KILLED. HER HEART WAS BROKEN INTO A GAZILLION PIECES.

LATER EVENING STAR MARRIED SOME OTHER GUY AND HAD CHILDREN. ONE OF THOSE CHILDREN HAD A CHILD WHO HAD A CHILD WHO HAD A CHILD WHO HAD DADDY WHO HAD ME. THAT IS HOW I AM RELATED TO HER. SHE IS MY FAVORITE RELATIVE.

EVENING STAR NEVER FORGOT RUNNING DEER. WHEN SHE WAS AN OLD LADY, SHE WENT TO WHERE HE WAS KILLED AND LEFT THE STAR NECKLACE THERE. IT WAS VERY SAD AND ROMANTIC.

THE END.

I looked up from my paper after I finished reading. All of the kids in Ms. Colman's class clapped hard.

I glanced at Ms. Colman. She was giving me a funny look.

"My goodness, Karen," said Ms. Colman. "That was very . . . interesting."

"Thank you," I said. I smiled at Ms. Colman and took my seat. I was pretty sure my report would go up on the workboard.

So far it had been one of the most interesting ones. Ms. Colman had said so.

I know that some of the things in my report were probably not one hundred percent true. But the thing was, no one knew for sure. No one could be certain that Evening Star had not had the life I wrote about. And if no one could say that she had not, then there was a chance she *had*. And a lot of the other details were things Mommy or Daddy had said — about the pumpkin and Highgate Hall. So it was not as if I were making them up or anything.

17

Field Day

The rest of the week rushed by. I Prepared myself for Field Day every day by Practicing with Hannie and Nancy. By Friday I had forgotten all about my ancestor report. I was thinking about one thing and one thing only: Field Day.

On Friday morning the weather was perfect — warm and clear. As soon as the teachers took attendance, all the students in Stoneybrook Academy gathered outside on the school field. I stood with the other kids in Ms. Colman's class and did stretching exercises to warm up.

I noticed Mommy in the bleachers. Next to her were Daddy and Andrew. Daddy had given me a ride to school that morning. Andrew had even skipped preschool. That is how important Field Day was.

Mommy, Daddy, and Andrew waved to me. I gave them a huge smile and waved back.

This was so exciting. Both Mommy and Daddy would be there to see my moment of victory over Pamela Harding. I was Prepared. I had Practiced. Now I was ready to Perform. I could imagine Mommy and Daddy shouting for joy as I won every event. They would be so Proud.

Soon Mrs. Mackey was blowing her whistle and organizing events.

Guess what. I did not win every event. In fact, I won only two events — the relay race (yea, Three Musketeers and Sara Ford!) and the wheelbarrow race (all that Practice with Nancy paid off).

But I came in second in three events and third in another. As we started the last event, I was leading in total points — but Pamela was just behind me.

The last event was the water-balloon toss with Ricky. If we could win this, I would be the highest-scoring person in my class. I would win the gift certificate. I decided I would share my new sports equipment with Ricky and Sara too.

Ricky and I took our spots for the first toss.

"Lob it nice and easy," I called to him.

Mrs. Mackey blew her whistle. Ricky tossed the water balloon to me. I caught it. It did not burst! (Hannie and Nancy's did. They were out on the first round. Boo.)

Ricky and I each took two giant steps backward.

"Careful," said Ricky.

"I will be," I said.

I threw the water balloon to him. Oh no! It was not a good toss. The balloon was blooping end over end. . . . *Splat!* It exploded all over Ricky.

I felt terrible. Not only were we out of the balloon toss, but my pretend husband was soaking wet. Ricky did not seem to mind, though. He was shaking himself and laughing.

My heart sank when I saw Pamela and Jannie grinning as they tossed their balloon back and forth. They ended up winning that event. Which gave Pamela the points she needed to tie with me.

I had not won, and she had not won. We were Field Day Co-champions.

I was about to say "Congratulations" to Pamela (I try to be polite, even to meanie-mos) when Pamela said, "See? I told you I would win."

"I told you I would win too," I shot back. "So there."

We glared at each other for a long, long moment. Then we looked away at the same time. We stomped off.

The glaring contest had ended just the way Field Day had — in a tie.

Oh, well. You cannot win them all. And with a person like Pamela, sometimes you cannot win any of them. The best you can do is tie.

Who Is Evening Star?

When the Field Day events were over, it was time for the awards. Ms. Colman gathered our class and all our parents in the middle of the school field. (Other classes were grouped around their teachers elsewhere on the field.) Andrew and I stood between Mommy and Daddy.

"This year we have two winners of Field Day," said Ms. Colman. "Karen Brewer and Pamela Harding tied for the most points. So they will split the gift certificate to Phil's Sporting Goods."

Ms. Colman called Pamela and me to her. She told us each to hold a corner of the gift certificate while our parents took photos of us smiling. I smiled extra big for Mommy and Daddy. Hannie and Nancy cheered for me.

I thought about my Packett and Brewer ancestors. None of them had won anything. And here I was, only seven years old, and already a winner of half a gift certificate. Just think of the things I would be winning when I was eight.

"Pamela, Karen," said Ms. Colman. "Since there are two of you and only one gift certificate, I will keep it for now. Tomorrow I will go to Phil's and turn it in for two gift certificates of equal value. Then I will give each of you one. Does that sound fair?"

Pamela and I nodded. I guessed Pamela would be able to buy only half a million pairs of goofy pom-pom socks.

"Okay, everybody," Ms. Colman said to my class and our parents. "The picnic is waiting for us. There are hot dogs, hamburgers, watermelon slices, chips, and drinks for everyone."

"Yea!" everyone (even the parents) shouted.

I ran back to Mommy, Daddy, and Andrew.

"Karen, we are so proud of you," said Daddy.

"All your hard work paid off," said Mommy. "You earned the burn."

I grinned. "I guess I did. But I really do not ever want to see that aerobics tape again."

Mommy and Daddy laughed.

"I want watermelon," said Andrew. He pointed at the table that held slices and slices of bright pink watermelon.

"Help yourself," said Daddy. "Just do not run off too far."

Andrew raced away.

I was about to suggest that we get some hot dogs when Ms. Colman walked over to us.

"Hello, Watson," said Ms. Colman. "Hi, Lisa. Thank you for coming to our Field Day."

"We would not have missed it," said Daddy.

"No, indeed," said Mommy.

"You must be very proud of Karen," said Ms. Colman.

"Oh, we are," said Mommy.

"She is a very special girl," said Daddy.

"I think so too," said Ms. Colman.

I beamed. I love this sort of conversation.

"And she comes from a very special family," said Ms. Colman. "The essay Karen wrote about her ancestor was fascinating."

Uh-oh. Suddenly I did not like where the conversation was heading.

"Oh really?" said Daddy. He turned to me. "I never asked you, Karen. Who did you finally decide to write about? Great-aunt Josephine? One of Mommy's ancestors?"

Mommy, Daddy, and Ms. Colman looked at me. They waited for me to answer. I did not want to, but I had to say something.

"Um, I am starving," I said. "I need a hot dog, right now. Come on, Ms. Colman. Let's go get something to eat."

I grabbed Ms. Colman's hand and tried to drag her away from Mommy and Daddy.

"Slow down, Karen," said Ms. Colman, laughing. Then she turned to Mommy and Daddy. "Karen's ancestor certainly sounded remarkable, but I was confused about one thing. Was Evening Star on your side of the family, Watson? Or on yours, Lisa?"

Daddy looked at Mommy. Mommy looked at Daddy.

I let go of Ms. Colman's hand. I wished I could disappear.

"Evening Star?" Daddy said. "There was nobody on my side of the family named Evening Star. Lisa?"

Mommy shook her head. "No Evening Stars among the Packetts."

Mommy, Daddy, and Ms. Colman turned back to me.

"Karen?" Daddy said.

"Yes?" I replied in a very small voice.

"Who is Evening Star?"

Gulp. I was in trouble now.

19

Karen Is Found Out

"Well, Karen?" Ms. Colman asked. "If Evening Star was not related to your father or your mother, who was she related to? Your stepmother or stepfather?"

That was an idea. I could say that Seth had told me about Evening Star. Or that Elizabeth had. But I would never get away with it. And then I would be in even more trouble.

As painful as it was, the truth would have to come out.

"Evening Star was one of Daddy's ancestors," I said.

Daddy looked surprised.

"Sort of," I added quickly. "Remember you told me that one of your ancestors was Cherokee?" I reminded him.

"I said she might have been Cherokee," Daddy said. "And I definitely did not tell you her name was Evening Star."

"Well, I added some details," I said. "To make the story more interesting."

"*Some* details?" Daddy said. "I did not give you *any* details about my possibly Cherokee ancestor. I do not know anything about her."

"You did not tell Karen that Evening Star was a pioneer woman who had been kidnapped by Cherokees?" asked Ms. Colman.

Daddy shook his head.

"You did not tell Karen that she fell in love with a man named Running Deer?" asked Ms. Colman.

Daddy shook his head.

"That he was killed protecting his people

from the army, that Evening Star never forgot him, and that when she was an old woman she put the star necklace he carved for her on his grave?"

Daddy started to shake his head, then stopped.

"Wait a second," he said. "That story sounds exactly like a movie Kristy was talking about. It was called *Morning Sky*."

Everyone looked at me. I felt my face turning red. My stomach hurt.

"Karen," said Ms. Colman. "Did you borrow your ancestor's story from a movie?"

I had not thought of it as borrowing. (I was glad Ms. Colman had not said "steal.") But that is what I had done.

"Hannie and Nancy had such interesting ancestors," I explained. "And all of my ancestors were boring. So I thought about how I probably had lots of ancestors who did great things — only nobody remembers them. Then I thought about Daddy's Cherokee great-great-grandmother. No one knew anything about her. And I figured she had to be pretty interesting. I thought about all the things she could have done. I did not mean to make everything up. It just sort of happened. I am sorry," I whispered.

For a few moments everyone was silent. Then Ms. Colman said, "Karen, a vivid imagination is a good thing to have — *most* of the time. But this report was supposed to stick to the facts. You were not supposed to make things up. It was wrong of you to present the report to our class and pretend that it was true. Do you understand?"

I nodded silently.

"All right. Now, first you must write your report over," said Ms. Colman. "And this time you must not let your imagination get the better of you. You must choose a real ancestor. A person does not have to be famous or glamorous to be important and interesting, you know. I am sure you can find a woman in your family to write about."

I nodded again. "Okay."

"Then you must write me a whole page on why what you did was wrong," continued Ms. Colman. "Not only wrong, but unfair to your classmates, who all used real ancestors."

"I understand," I said. I was gigundoly embarrassed. I could hardly even be excited about co-winning Field Day.

But I knew Ms. Colman was right.

I sighed. "The punishment is fair," I said.

20

The Three Musketeers

Andrew came running to us then, holding a humongous hunk of watermelon. "I am on my fourth piece," he said, and spat out a seed.

All of a sudden I was starving.

"May I go now?" I asked Mommy and Daddy. "If I do not have a hot dog soon, I am going to faint."

Daddy smiled. "Well, we do not want you to pass out. You may go."

I waved good-bye to Mommy, Daddy, and

Ms. Colman and went to find Hannie and Nancy.

But first I had to eat something.

Mrs. Mackey was roasting hot dogs on a grill. A bunch of kids were crowded around, waiting to be served.

Tweet! "Line up, people!" yelled Mrs. Mackey.

Good old Mrs. Mackey. I got in line, and pretty soon I had my hot dog. Mmm, mmm! There is nothing more delicious than a grilled hot dog when you are starving.

I saw Hannie and Nancy across the field and ran to them.

"Hi, Karen!" Hannie called. "I saw your parents with Ms. Colman. What were they talking about?"

"My ancestor report," I said. "I sort of invented some things about my ancestor." I was too embarrassed to tell them how much I had invented.

"You did?" said Nancy. "Really?"

"Yes," I said. "All of my real ancestors

were boring. So I made one up that was interesting."

Nancy and Hannie looked at each other.

Then Hannie said, "You know, Karen, I figured you had made some of that stuff up. I kind of believed about the pumpkin and the skiing, but the ship that sank was just too much."

Nancy nodded. "Yes," she said. "And the story of how your ancestor was kidnapped by Native Americans and fell in love sounded a lot like that movie *Morning Sky*. I wondered if you borrowed parts of your story from it."

"You knew all along?" I asked my friends.

They nodded. "Pretty much," said Nancy.

"Well, it is a lot harder to fool you than some other people," I said, laughing.

"That is right," said Hannie. "And you should not forget it."

"One thing is for sure, Karen," said Nancy. "When your great-great-granddaughter has to write a report on an interesting ances-

tor, she will have lots to write about."

"All she will have to do is ask about you," said Hannie.

Nancy and Hannie laughed.

I could not help it. I had to laugh too.

L. GODWIN

About the Author

ANN M. MARTIN lives in New York City and loves animals, especially cats. She has two cats of her own, Gussie and Woody.

Other books by Ann M. Martin that you might enjoy are *Stage Fright*; *Me and Katie (the Pest)*; and the books in *The Baby-sitters Club* series.

Ann likes ice cream and *I Love Lucy*. And she has her own little sister, whose name is Jane.

Little Sister

Don't miss #109

KAREN'S SHOW AND SHARE

What else could I say about it? What would make it a better Show and Share? My classmates were being a tough audience. I could not stand it. I wanted them to ooh and aah, just the way I had for them.

Suddenly I blurted out, "I have met Bobby Martinez." I do not know where that came from. It just popped out of my mouth.

Terri stopped fidgeting.

"I have met him more than once," I said, listening to myself in amazement.

Jannie looked up from her doodle.

"He is a friend of mine," I said. My eyes were wide. My heart was pounding. What was I doing?

Ricky's mouth was still wide open. But he was not yawning anymore. His mouth was open in wonder.